Iris and Walter

Iris and Walter

WRITTEN BY

Elissa Haden Guest

ILLUSTRATED BY

Christine Davenier

GULLIVER BOOKS
HARCOURT, INC.
SAN DIEGO NEW YORK LONDON

For Nick and Gena and Nathanael, with all my love,
and for my beloved father, in memory   —E. H. G

For Philippe Rouault   —C. D.

www.harcourt.com

First Gulliver Books paperback edition 2002
Gulliver Books is a registered trademark of Harcourt, Inc., registered in
the United States of America and/or other jurisdictions.

Library of Congress Cataloging-in-Publication Data
Guest, Elissa Haden.
Iris and Walter/Elissa Haden Guest; illustrations by Christine Davenier.
p.   cm.
"Gulliver Books."
Summary: When Iris moves to the country, she misses the city where
she formerly lived; but with the help of a new friend named Walter, she
learns to adjust to her new home.
[1. Country life—Fiction.   2. City and town life—Fiction.
3. Friendship—Fiction.]   I. Davenier, Christine, ill.   II. Title.
PZ7.G9375Ir   2000
[E]—dc21   99-6242
ISBN 0-15-202122-1
ISBN 0-15-216442-1 (pb)

I H G F E D C B
H G F E D C B A (pb)

PRINTED IN SINGAPORE

Contents

1. Moving

When Iris and Iris's family moved
from the big city to the country,
Iris was sad.

She missed her noisy street.
She missed her wide front stoop.

She missed playing baseball after supper
until it was too dark to see the ball.

Iris missed the long hallway
where she roller-skated on rainy days.

And at night she missed the tango music
from apartment 3B.

She missed the *whoosh* of the bus doors
opening and closing.
She missed the *rumble-rumble* of the subway
under the ground.
Iris missed her old life.
Iris missed her old life in the big city.

2. Cheer Up

"Cheer up, my Iris," said Iris's mother.
"We're in the country now.
Why don't you run around
and do a cartwheel in the grass?"
But Iris did not want to run around.
Iris did not want to do a cartwheel
in the grass.

So Iris's mother ran around.
Iris's mother did a cartwheel in the grass.

"Talk about fun!" said Iris's mother.
"Hmm," said Iris.

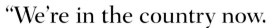

"Cheer up, my Iris," said Iris's father.
"We're in the country now.
Why don't you play monkeys
and swing from the tall trees?"

But Iris did not want to play monkeys.
Iris did not want to swing from the tall trees.

So Iris's father played monkeys.
Iris's father swung from the tall trees.
"Talk about fun!" said Iris's father.
"Hmm," said Iris.

"Iris, my girl," said Grandpa.
Iris hoped he would not say "Cheer up."
He did not. Grandpa said,
"Let's you and I go for a walk."
Iris smiled.
And off they went.

3. A Walk and a Talk

Iris and Grandpa went for a walk.
"Can I tell you something?"
Iris asked.
"You may tell me anything,"
said Grandpa.
"I hate the country," said Iris.
"Why?" asked Grandpa.
"Because there are no children
here," said Iris. "The country is
as lonely as Mars."

"Iris, my girl, there must be
some children somewhere," said Grandpa.
"Do you think so?" asked Iris.
"I *know* so. We shall have to find them, Iris.
We shall be explorers!"

Iris and Grandpa
walked down the road.
The birds were singing.
The roses were blooming.
And around the bend,
someone was waiting.

Iris and Grandpa walked around the bend.
They saw a great big green tree.
"What a tree!" said Grandpa.
"So green!" said Iris.
"So beautiful," said Grandpa.
"I want to climb it," said Iris.

Down came a ladder.

"Amazing! I wonder
what's up there?"
said Grandpa.
"I'll go see," said Iris.
Iris began to climb.
"How is it up there?"
called Grandpa.
"It's very green!" yelled Iris.
Iris climbed higher and higher
until she was almost at the top
of the great big green tree.

"Grandpa?!" called Iris.
"There's a house up here."
"Amazing!" said Grandpa.

Iris knocked on the door.
"Come in," said a voice.
Iris opened the door.
"Hi, I'm Walter," said Walter.
"I'm Iris," said Iris.
Iris and Walter shook hands.
"Hey, Grandpa, there's a kid up here
named Walter!" yelled Iris.
"How wonderful," said Grandpa.
And it was.

WALTER

4. A New Life

Iris and Walter played every day.
They climbed trees.
They rolled down hills.
They played hide-and-seek.

When it rained,
Walter showed Iris his hat collection.
And Iris showed Walter
how to roller-skate—indoors.

Some days they rode
Walter's sweet pony, Sal.
Other days they sat on a fence
and watched a horse named Rain
running wild.

"Tell me about the big city," said Walter.
"Well," said Iris, "in the big city,
there are lots and lots and lots of people."
"Ah," said Walter. "But in the country
there are lots and lots and lots of stars."

Iris and Walter played every day.
But still Iris dreamed of the big city.
She dreamed of her noisy street
and her wide front stoop.

She dreamed of tango music and of
roller-skating down long hallways.
But Iris was not sad.

For in the country, there were red-tailed hawks and starry skies.

There were pale roses.
And there was cool grass beneath her feet.
There was a wild horse named Rain
and a sweet pony named Sal.

And across the meadow,
over the stream, high in a tree,
was a little house.
And inside there was
a new friend . . . Walter.

43

The illustrations in this book were created in
pen and ink on keacolor paper.
The display type was set in Elroy.
The text type was set in Fairfield Medium.
Printed and bound by Tien Wah Press, Singapore
Production supervision by Sandra Grebenar and
Wendi Taylor
Designed by Kaelin Chappell